HAROLD and the DINOSAUR MYSTERY

Written by Erica Frost

Illustrated by Deborah Sims

Troll Associates

Troll Associates

Library of Congress Catalog Card Number: 78-60123
ISBN 0-89375-076-X

10 9 8 7 6 5 4

HAROLD and the DINOSAUR MYSTERY

On Berry Street, almost everyone had a
pet.

Patty had Poppy.

Iris had Irma.

Donald had Dimples. And that's not all.

Mary had Muffin.

Richard had Rosie and Rudolph.

Carol had Cupcake. And . . .

Harold had Henry.

Why, then, did everyone make such a
fuss about Henry?

"He's ugly!" said Iris.

"He's too big!" said Richard.

"I don't trust him!" said Mary.

They told Harold to get a dog or a cat or a mouse or a rat or a monkey or a donkey or a snake or a bird.

"Even a skunk would be better than Henry!" said Donald.

"Anything would be better than a *dinosaur*!" said Iris.

"What's wrong with a dinosaur?" asked Harold.

"Whoever heard of a dinosaur for a pet?" sniffed Carol.

"Nobody else has a dinosaur," said Richard.

"Henry is a very smart dinosaur," said Harold. "He is loyal. He is kind. And he is my friend."

"Then you are a dope," said Donald.

And everyone said: "Yes, you are a dope. And Henry is a dope, too!"

They stuck out their tongues, and made fun of Harold and his pet. Then they turned on their heels and walked away.

From then on, everyone crossed the street when they saw Harold. They didn't save a place for him on line anymore. They didn't ask him to join their clubs. It wasn't easy for Harold and Henry.

But sometimes it wasn't so hard, either.
On the day of the big parade, Harold had the
best seat.

When the apples were ripe in Lark Meadow, Harold picked the biggest and reddest and juiciest ones.

And he always got to school before the school bus. (Henry could be very speedy when he wanted to be.)

Then one day, something mysterious happened. Poppy disappeared. Nobody knew where she was. Everyone on Berry Street was out looking for her.

Everyone, except Harold. Harold wanted to help, but he was afraid they would call him a dope. He was afraid they would tell him to go away. So he sat on Henry's head, and watched.

Patty looked under the front porch.

Iris looked up in the trees.

Donald and Mary checked every backyard.

And Richard and Carol looked everywhere else.

Nobody found Poppy. She was gone.

"Henry ate her up," said Carol.

"He gobbled her up in the middle of the night!" said Mary.

"Oh, poor, poor Poppy!" cried Patty.

"Henry is a monster!" cried Richard. "Harold should give him away!"

"Yes! Yes!" they all shouted. "Harold must give Henry away!"

Off they marched to Harold's house. Harold was in his garden. He was planting a blackberry bush for Henry.

"Henry is a monster!" cried Mary.

"He ate my poor Poppy!" sobbed Patty.

"He is a blight on the neighborhood!" said Richard, who liked to show off with big words.

"Don't be silly," said Harold. "Henry eats fruits and flowers. He eats berries and seeds. He would never, never eat a cat!"

But nobody listened to Harold. "Give him away!" they shouted. "Give him away!"

Then Harold told them how gentle Henry was.

"He wouldn't harm a flea," said Harold. "Believe me. Henry did not eat Poppy."

The children mumbled and grumbled. "We will give him one more chance," they said. "But there had better not be any more trouble!"

Then they turned on their heels and
walked away.

But the very next day, there was more trouble. Dimples and Muffin were missing. Nobody knew where they were. Nobody knew where to find them. Things did not look good for Henry.

"We should have tied him up!" cried Mary.

"We should have hit him with a stick!" cried Donald.

"We were too kind," said Iris.

Everyone was very angry. They went to see Harold again. He was at work in his tree house. Henry was helping.

"Where is Dimples?" asked Donald.

"I want my Muffin!" said Mary.

And Richard, who had just finished
reading a book about pirates, hollered:
"Avast, you scurvy bloke! Turn loose the

prisoners or prepare to walk the plank!"

"Don't be silly," said Harold. "I don't have any prisoners."

"Of course not," said Iris. "Henry ate them all!"

Mary pointed to a rag doll that was lying in the grass. "Where did you get that?" she asked.

"Henry found it," said Harold. "He brought it home this morning."

"Hah!" cried Mary. "Do you expect me to believe that? That doll belonged to Muffin! Oh! Poor, poor Muffin!"

"You are making a terrible mistake," said Harold. "Henry is innocent."

"Prove it!" said Donald.

"Yes, prove it!" said Mary.

And they all cried: "Prove it! Prove it! Prove it!"

"I will," said Harold. "Henry and I will get to the bottom of this. You'll see!"

The children mumbled and grumbled. "All right," they said. "You have until tomorrow morning!"

Then they turned on their heels and walked away.

Harold patted Henry's tail. "Don't worry, old friend," he said. "We will solve this mystery. We must."

That night, when everyone was asleep, Harold crept out of the house. Henry was waiting for him. Softly, they tiptoed across the grass. Then they waited behind a tree, where they could see all the houses on Berry Street.

The silver moon cast long, dark shadows. Everything was still.

Suddenly, there was a sound. Henry sat up straight. But it was only a dog howling at the moon.

The stars winked at them. Then something stirred. Henry stretched his long neck and looked around. But it was only the wind sighing in the trees.

Then, they heard another sound. *Tap,*
tap, tap . . .

Coming down the street was a little old
man. He walked with the help of a crooked
stick. Tap, tap, tap . . . slowly, he came down
Berry Street, carrying a big sack.

Harold and Henry watched him.

The old man poked here. He poked
there. He peered into the darkness, and
peeped down the alleys.

"I wonder what he wants," whispered
Harold.

The old man stopped at Richard's
house. He looked around him. He did not
see Harold and Henry hiding behind the
tree. He did not know that they were
watching his every move.

Then, the old man stepped into the darkness. Harold could not see him, but he could hear his stick . . . tap, tap, tap.

When he stepped back into the moon-
light, the sack was on his back. It was full. It
was bumpy. And the bumps were moving!

"I think he has Rosie and Rudolph!"
whispered Harold. "Hurry, Henry! We have
to be sure!"

Harold and Henry galloped down Berry
Street. They turned into Richard's yard.
Harold went straight to the rabbit hutch. It
was empty. Rosie and Rudolph were gone!

They looked for the old man. They did
not see him. He had disappeared into the
shadows.

"We have to find him!" cried Harold.
"We have to find the old man to prove that
you are innocent!"

The next morning, Richard could not
find his rabbits. Rosie and Rudolph were
gone. And Henry's footprints were
everywhere!

Richard called the others. He showed them the footprints.

"Dinosaur tracks!" said Donald.
"Henry!" said Iris.
"This is the last straw!" said Richard.

They ran all the way to Harold's house.
They marched up to his door.

"Look!" said Carol. "A note." She read it
aloud:

Dear Friends,
  Meet me at 21 Blackbird
Lane. I will tell you the
answer to the mystery.
      Sincerely yours,
            Harold

"Suppose it's a trick," said Iris.
"It better not be," said Patty.
"Let's go!" said Donald.

They marched down Berry Street, up
Willow Way, and across Robin Road. At last,
they came to Blackbird Lane.

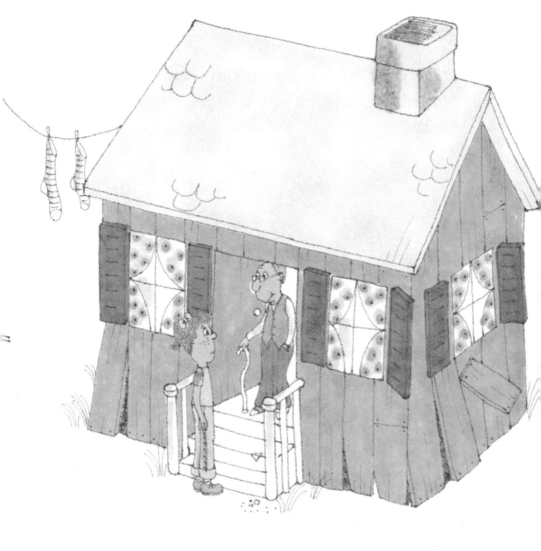

Number 21 Blackbird Lane was a
tumbledown cottage. Mary rang the bell. An
old man came to the door. He was leaning
on a crooked stick.

"Come in," he said. "Come right inside."
He led the children into a small, cheerful
room.

Rosie and Rudolph were sitting on a
table. Rosie was munching a carrot. Rudolph
was nibbling a lettuce leaf. They were safe
and sound.

Poppy was purring in front of the fire.

Muffin was chewing a meaty bone. He wagged his tail when he saw Mary.

Dimples was preening his feathers. He squawked and bowed to Donald.

Harold and Henry were there, too.

"This is Mr. Sprinkle," said Harold. "He is a very lonely person. Now that he is old, no one comes to visit him anymore."

"That is why I wanted Poppy and Muffin and Dimples and Rosie and Rudolph to live with me," said Mr. Sprinkle. "But now I'm very sorry. Harold told me how much you miss your pets."

"If it weren't for Henry, I would never have found Mr. Sprinkle," said Harold. "Henry followed his trail. He's very smart."

"Harold and Henry are real heroes," said Mr. Sprinkle. He patted Harold on the head.

Everyone agreed with Mr. Sprinkle. They asked Harold to please be their friend again. Harold said okay, but only if Henry could be their friend, too.

Then Richard said that when Rosie had babies, he would give two little rabbits to Mr. Sprinkle.

Patty promised to give him one of Poppy's kittens.

And Mary said he could certainly have
one of Muffin's puppies. Someday. If Muffin
ever had puppies.

Then Mr. Sprinkle served apple juice and cookies. It was just like a party. Everyone had a very good time.

When it was time to go, they promised to come again. They promised to visit Mr. Sprinkle whenever they could.

And they did.